This book belongs to:
MAIR
BROWN
D0783663

A catalogue record for this book is available from the British Library
Published by Ladybird Books Ltd
80 Strand London WC2R 0RL
A Penguin Company
012 - 15 14 13 12

ISBN: 978-1-84646-975-6
Printed in China

Chicken Licken

Retold by Vera Southgate M.A., B.Com
with illustrations by Peter Barrett

Ladybird *tales*

Once upon a time, there was a little chicken called Chicken Licken. One day an acorn fell from a tree and hit Chicken Licken on the head.

Chicken Licken thought that the sky was falling down. So he ran off to tell the king.

On the way, Chicken Licken met Henny Penny.

"Good morning, Chicken Licken," said Henny Penny. "Where are you going in such a hurry?"

“Oh! Henny Penny!” said Chicken Licken. “The sky is falling down and I’m on my way to tell the king.”

“Then I’d better go with you,” said Henny Penny.

So Chicken Licken and Henny Penny hurried on, to tell the king that the sky was falling down.

On the way, Chicken Licken and Henny Penny met Cocky Locky.

"Good morning, Chicken Licken," said Cocky Locky. "Where are you two going in such a hurry?"

"Oh! Cocky Locky!" said Chicken Licken. "The sky is falling down and we are on our way to tell the king."

"Then I'd better go with you," said Cocky Locky.

So Chicken Licken, Henny Penny and Cocky Locky hurried on, to tell the king that the sky was falling down.

On the way, Chicken Licken, Henny Penny and Cocky Locky met Ducky Lucky.

"Good morning, Chicken Licken," said Ducky Lucky. "Where are you all going in such a hurry?"

"Oh! Ducky Lucky!" said Chicken Licken. "The sky is falling down and we are on our way to tell the king."

"Then I'd better go with you," said Ducky Lucky.

So Chicken Licken, Henny Penny, Cocky Locky and Ducky Lucky hurried on, to tell the king that the sky was falling down.

On the way, Chicken Licken, Henny Penny, Cocky Locky and Ducky Lucky met Drakey Lakey.

"Good morning, Chicken Licken," said Drakey Lakey. "Where are you all going in such a hurry?"

"Oh! Drakey Lakey!" said Chicken Licken. "The sky is falling down and we are on our way to tell the king."

"Then I'd better go with you," said Drakey Lakey.

So Chicken Licken, Henny Penny, Cocky Locky, Ducky Lucky and Drakey Lakey hurried on, to tell the king that the sky was falling down.

On the way, Chicken Licken, Henny Penny, Cocky Locky, Ducky Lucky and Drakey Lakey met Goosey Loosey.

"Good morning, Chicken Licken," said Goosey Loosey. "Where are you all going in such a hurry?"

"Oh! Goosey Loosey!" said Chicken Licken. "The sky is falling down and we are on our way to tell the king."

"Then I'd better go with you," said Goosey Loosey.

So Chicken Licken, Henny Penny, Cocky Locky, Ducky Lucky, Drakey Lakey and Goosey Loosey hurried on, to tell the king that the sky was falling down.

On the way, Chicken Licken, Henny Penny, Cocky Locky, Ducky Lucky, Drakey Lakey and Goosey Loosey met Turkey Lurkey.

"Good morning, Chicken Licken," said Turkey Lurkey. "Where are you all going in such a hurry?"

"Oh! Turkey Lurkey!" said Chicken Licken. "The sky is falling down and we are on our way to tell the king."

"Then I'd better go with you," said Turkey Lurkey.

So Chicken Licken, Henny Penny, Cocky Locky, Ducky Lucky, Drakey Lakey, Goosey Loosey and Turkey Lurkey hurried on, to tell the king that the sky was falling down.

On the way, Chicken Licken, Henny Penny, Cocky Locky, Ducky Lucky, Drakey Lakey, Goosey Loosey and Turkey Lurkey met Foxy Loxy.

"Good morning, Chicken Licken," said Foxy Loxy. "Where are you all going in such a hurry?"

"Oh! Foxy Loxy!" said Chicken Licken. "The sky is falling down and we are on our way to tell the king."

"I know where to find the king," said Foxy Loxy. "You had better all follow me."

So Chicken Licken, Henny Penny, Cocky Locky, Ducky Lucky, Drakey Lakey, Goosey Loosey and Turkey Lurkey followed Foxy Loxy.

Foxy Loxy led them straight into his den, where his wife and their little foxes were waiting for their dinners.

Then the foxes ate Chicken Licken, Henny Penny, Cocky Locky, Ducky Lucky, Drakey Lakey, Goosey Loosey and Turkey Lurkey for their dinners.

So Chicken Licken never found the king to tell him that he thought the sky was falling down.

mini
Beauty and the Beast
Ladybird tales

mini
Cinderella
Ladybird tales

mini
Hansel and Gretel
Ladybird tales

mini
The Princess and the Pea
Ladybird tales

mini
Puss in Boots
Ladybird tales

mini
Sleeping Beauty
Ladybird tales

mini
The Three Billy Goats Gruff
Ladybird tales

mini
The Three Little Pigs
Ladybird tales

mini
Dick Whittington
Ladybird tales

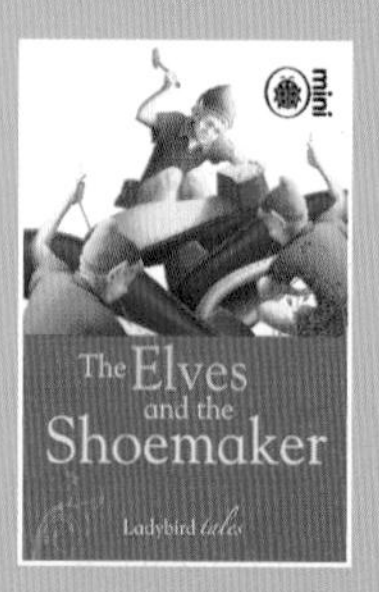
mini
The Elves and the Shoemaker
Ladybird tales

mini
The Little Red Hen
Ladybird tales

mini
Snow White and the Seven Dwarfs
Ladybird tales